MR. SLOW

by Roger Hargreaves

WORLD INTERNATIONAL
MANCHESTER

Mr Slow, as you might well know, or maybe you don't, lived next door to Mr Busy.

He'd built his house himself.

Slowly.

It had taken him ten years!

And, as you might well know, or maybe you don't, Mr Slow talked in an extraordinarily slow way.

He . . . talked . . . like . . . this.

And every single thing he did was as slow as the way he talked.

For instance.

If Mr Slow was writing this book about himself, you wouldn't be able to read it yet.

He wouldn't even have got as far as this page!

For instance.

If Mr Slow was eating a currant cake for tea, it took him until bedtime.

He'd eat it crumb by crumb, currant by currant, chewing each crumb and each currant one hundred times.

For instance.

Last Christmas, it took Mr Slow until New Year's Day to open his Christmas presents.

And then it took him until Easter to write his thank-you letters!

Oh, he was a slow man.

Now, this story isn't about the time Mr Slow went on a picnic with Mr Busy.

That's another story.

No, this story is about the time Mr Slow decided to get a job.

He read all the job advertisements in the Sunday paper (which took him until Wednesday) and then he went and got himself a job reading the news on television.

Can you imagine?

It was very embarrassing!

"Good . . . evening . . .," said Mr Slow. "Here . . . is . . . the . . . nine . . . o' . . . clock . . . news."

It took him until midnight to read it!

And everybody who was watching went to sleep.

So, that job wasn't any good.

Was it?

Then, Mr Slow got himself a job as a taxi driver.

"Take me to the railway station," cried Mr Uppity, as he leapt into his taxi. "I have a train to catch at 3 o'clock!"

"Right . . . ho," said Mr Slow, and set off.

At one mile an hour!

And arrived at the station at 4 o'clock.

So, that job wasn't any good.

Was it?

And, that summer, Mr Slow got a job making ice cream. But, by the time he'd made the ice cream, it wasn't exactly the right sort of weather to be selling ice cream!

Brrr!

So, Mr Slow got himself a job making woolly scarves. But, by the time he'd finished making the scarves, it wasn't exactly the right sort of weather to be selling scarves!

Phew!

Poor Mr Slow.

He went around to ask the other Mr Men what he should do.

"Be a racing driver!" suggested Mr Silly.

Can you imagine?

No!

"Be an engine driver!" suggested Mr Funny.

Can you imagine?

No! No!

"Be a speedboat driver!" suggested Mr Tickle.

Can you imagine?

No! No! No!

But then, Mr Happy had an extremely good idea.

Most sensible.

"Be a steamroller driver," he suggested.

And today that is exactly what Mr Slow does.

Slowly backwards and slowly forwards he drives.

Up and down.

Down and up.

Ever so slowly.

The next time you see a steamroller doing that, look and see if Mr Slow is driving it.

If he is, you shout to him, "Hello, Mr Slow! Are you having a nice time?"

And he'll wave, and shout back to you.

"Yes . . . thank . . . you . . .," he'll shout.

"Good . . . bye!"

SPECIAL OFFERS FOR MR MEN AND LITTLE MISS READERS

In every Mr Men and Little Miss book you will find a special token.
Collect only six tokens and we will send you a super poster of your choice
featuring all your favourite Mr Men or Little Miss friends.

And for the first 4,000 readers we hear from, we will send you a
Mr Men activity pad* and a bookmark* as well – absolutely free!

Return this page with six tokens from Mr Men and/or Little Miss books to:
Marketing Department, World International Publishing, Egmont House,
PO Box 111, 61 Great Ducie Street, Manchester M60 3BL.

Your name:_____

Address:_____

_____

_____ Postcode: _____

Signature of parent or guardian: _____

I enclose **six** tokens – please send me a Mr Men poster ☐
I enclose **six** tokens – please send me a Little Miss poster ☐

We may occasionally wish to advise you of other children's books that
we publish. If you would rather we didn't, please tick this box ☐

*while stocks last   (Please note: this offer is limited to a maximum of two posters per household.)

Collect six of these tokens.
You will find one inside every
Mr Men and Little Miss book
which has this special offer.

1 TOKEN

JOIN THE MR MEN & LITTLE MISS CLUB

Treat your child to membership of the long-awaited Mr Men & Little Miss Club and see their delight when they receive a personal letter from Mr Happy and Little Miss Giggles together with a great value Welcome Pack.

In the Pack they'll discover a unique collection of items for learning and fun: their own personal membership card; a club badge **with their name on**; an exclusive club members' cassette tape with two Mr Men stories and four songs; a copy of the excellent Fun To Learn™ Mr Men magazine; a great Mr Men sticker book; their own tiny flock model of Mr Happy; a club pencil; and, from the superb Mr Men range, a diary (with a padlock), an amazing bendy pen, an eraser, a book mark, and a key ring!

And that's not all. On their birthday and again at Christmas they'll get a card from the Mr Men and Little Misses. And every month the Mr Men magazine (available from newsagents) features exclusive offers for club members.

If all this could be bought in the shops you would expect to pay at least £12.00. But a year's membership is superb value at just **£7.99** (plus 70p postage). To enrol your child please send **your** name, address and telephone number together with **your child's** full name, date of birth and address (including postcode) and a cheque or postal order for £8.69 (payable to Mr Men & Little Miss Club) to: Mr Happy, Happyland (Dept. WI), PO Box 142, Horsham RH13 5FJ. Or call 01403 242727 to pay by credit card.